llama llama mad at mama

Anna Dewdney

VIKING

P9-CJW-601

Llama Llama
having fun.
Blocks and puzzles
in the sun.

Time to shop!
It's Saturday!
Llama Llama
wants to **play**.

First the
shopping,
then a treat.
Mama Llama
gets the seat.

Llama dreaming
in the car—

Wake up! Wake up!
Here we are!

Great big building,
great big signs.
Lots of aisles,
lots of lines.

Llama Llama
out with Mama
shopping at the Shop-O-Rama.

SALE!
50 % OFF
BLUE DOT

SALE!
SALE!
SALE!

Yucky music,
great big feet.
Ladies smelling way too sweet.
Look at knees and stand in line.

Llama Llama
starts to **whine.**

SALE
20%OFF

Clearance sales
and discount buys.
What is little llama's size?
Try it on and take it off.
Pull and wiggle,
itch and cough.

Shirts and jackets,
pants and shoes.
Does this sweater
come in blue?
Brand-new socks
and underwear?

Llama Llama does not care.

Cheezee Puffs and Oatie Crunch.
What would llama like for lunch?
Llama Llama doesn't know.
Llama Llama wants to **go.**

Loaf of bread
and Cream of Wheat.
Llama Llama wants his treat.
It's no fun at Shop-O-Rama.
Llama Llama
MAD at Mama!

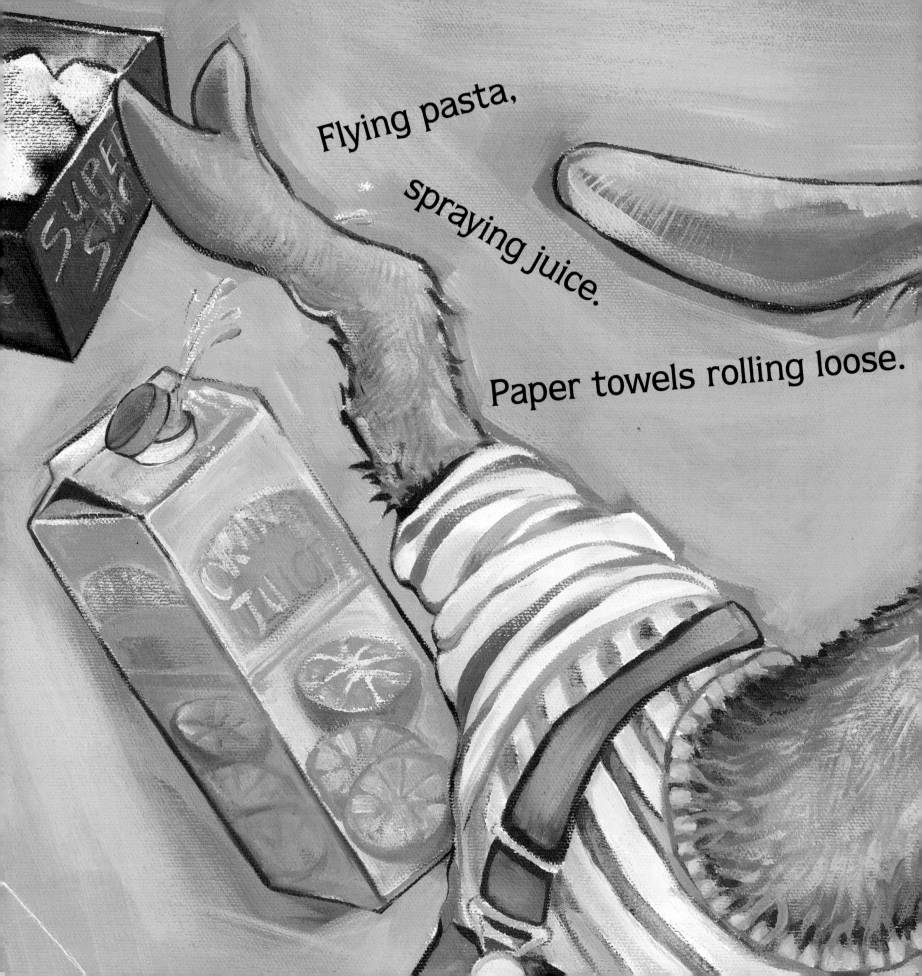

Coffee, bread, and chips galore.
Shoes and sweaters hit the floor.

CRASH the cart and SMASH the signs.
No more waiting! No more lines!
Out go socks and Cheezee Puffs. . . .

**Llama Llama,
that's enough!**

Please stop fussing, little llama.
No more of this **llama drama.**
I think shopping's boring, too—
but at least I'm here with **you.**

Let's see if we can make this fun **and** get the llama shopping done.

Let's be a team at Shop-O-Rama—
Llama Llama shops **with** Mama!

Sweep up pasta,
mop up juice.
Wrap up towels rolling loose.

Pick up puffs and find the socks.
Put the shoes back in the box.

Push the cart with Mama Llama,
almost done at Shop-O-Rama.

Time to leave.
The shopping's done.
No more waiting.
Time for fun.

Out to parking, not too far.
Where did Mama leave the car?

Snap the buckle,
grab the box.
Put on brand-new
shoes and socks.

Say good-bye to Shop-O-Rama.

Llama Llama
loves his mama.

For Cordelia, my shopping buddy

VIKING

Published by Penguin Group

Penguin Young Readers Group, 345 Hudson Street, New York, New York 10014, U.S.A.

Penguin Group (Canada), 90 Eglinton Avenue East, Suite 700, Toronto, Ontario, Canada M4P 2Y3

Penguin Books Ltd, Registered Offices: 80 Strand, London WC2R 0RL, England

First published in 2007 by Viking, a division of Penguin Young Readers Group

25 27 29 30 28 26 24

Copyright © Anna Dewdney, 2007

All rights reserved

LIBRARY OF CONGRESS CATALOGING-IN-PUBLICATION DATA

Dewdney, Anna.

Llama Llama mad at mama / by Anna Dewdney.

p. cm.

Summary: A young llama wants to play but must go shopping with his mother instead,

and so he gets angry and makes a mess at the store.

ISBN 978-0-670-06240-9 (hardcover)

[1. Mother and child—Fiction. 2. Shopping—Fiction. 3. Llamas—Fiction. 4. Stories in rhyme.] I. Title.

PZ8.3.D498Lkr 2007

[E]—dc22

2006037476

Printed in the United States of America

Set in ITC Quorum

31901061178184